THE LEGEND OF RIGEL
Hero dog of the Titanic

By Christine Jamesson

Illustrations by Lisa Sweet

DISCLAIMER

This is a story based on a tragic event in history.
Some names and stories have been changed, added or omitted.

First published by AuthorHouse 11/29/05

ISBN: 1-4208-8679-7 (sc)

Printed in the United States of America
Bloomington, Indiana

This book is printed on acid-free paper.

authorHOUSE

1663 LIBERTY DRIVE
BLOOMINGTON, INDIANA 47403
(800) 839-8640
www.authorhouse.com

DEDICATION

To Brianna, CJ

To Mary Henderson for your help and support, LS

ABOUT THE BREED

Newfoundlands are huge dogs that were originally bred to help fishermen with their duties. Their natural adaptations make it possible for them to swim in frigid water for extended periods of time. They are frequently used as ship's mascots because of their tremendous swimming ability and natural desire to rescue drowning victims.

The Mystery and Legend of Rigel

This book is a fictionalized account of one of the worst maritime disasters of the 20th century. Many stories and legends have been passed down about the Titanic. One in particular has been proclaimed true by some and a complete myth by others. That is the case with Rigel. There were two accounts of Rigel, both reported to be factual soon after the sinking in 1912. The first was published in the "New York Herald on April 21st, 1912. The second account was in the book called "Sinking of the Titanic and Great Sea Disasters" Copyright 1912. His story has resurfaced on several web-sites and has spurned heated debates on message boards as to whether he did or did not exist. All of the "official" inquiries make no mention of him or his new owner at all nor did any of the survivors. In spite of the argument regarding his existence one thing is certain. If any dog breed could perform the remarkable feat of surviving a long distance swim in freezing water it could only be a Newfoundland.

1. THE NEW ASSIGNMENT

It was April 10th and Rigel and his master were busy getting ready for their new assignment, crewmates on the beautiful new ship, the Titanic. Rigel's master was an officer on the ship while Rigel held the very important positions as mascot and water rescue dog. So far in his life he had only served as a mascot but little did he know that in a few days his rescue abilities would be tested to their limits!

Being a Newfoundland dog he loved the water and would always look forward to a long refreshing swim. Newfoundland's were built to be long distance swimmers with their huge webbed feet, thick water repellant fur, a powerful breaststroke and a tail which acts as a rudder. So who could be a better ship's mascot?

The Titanic deserved the best for no one had ever seen such a magnificent ship, it was the biggest and grandest of them all!

Walking up the gangplank, Rigel was filled with a sense of awe at the beauty and majesty of his newly assigned ship.

It was so unlike any other ship he had ever been on. The size, the decorations, the people, everything was so different and wonderful that Rigel thought himself one very lucky dog!

Rigel's master would miss most of the days events as he was on the night shift, but Rigel was allowed the run of the ship. Just as the Titanic was ready to start her voyage when an event happened that was an omen of things to come. As the Titanic started away from the dock, its massive propellers created so much suction that another steamship called the "New York" was torn away from its position. Its mooring ropes snapped like twigs and it was heading straight for the Titanic! People on the top deck started to scream, Rigel stood up against the rail to see what was happening.

"Oh no, he thought." He started to bark orders just as two tugs slipped in between the ships, stopping a disaster from happening. Rigel breathed a sigh of relief, but the people on board began to whisper that the ship was jinxed!

2.   MAKING THE ROUNDS

It has been two days now and the Titanic is well into her cruise. As Rigel walks along the deck, he hears the band practicing. "Hey big fella come here", they call. "We need an audience." Rigel enjoyed listening to music so he politely obeyed. Soon the soothing music and lull of the ship affected him and he started to drift off into a deep sleep. He was awakened by the band members' laughter, "now what kind of a critic are you? "Our music isn't supposed to put you to sleep!" Well boys, I guess we had better play ragtime and dance numbers or our guests will be asleep in their dinner plates!" They jumped into a snappy dance just as Rigel heard his name being called.

It was his master calling, his shift was beginning and he wanted Rigel by his side. The bridge was a familiar sight. Here he would keep a constant watch for danger. Two children stopped by and were full of questions.

Weighing in at over 150 pounds, they had never seen such a big dog in their life. "Oh he's beautiful, what's his name," they asked. "Why is he so big, he looks more like a bear!" Rigel's master patiently answered all their questions. "Rigel has to be big to be able to save people from drowning, now if you were drowning who do you think would be better at saving you; Rigel or a or a little terrier?" The children laughed and felt safer knowing that there was a dog "lifeguard" on duty.

There wasn't much for him to do on the bridge, so Rigel went on the top deck to make his daily rounds. The sky was clear and starry. The crisp coolness of the night air felt good against his thick fur. The ship was filled with happiness, people were dancing in the ballroom, young honeymoon couples were holding hands and admiring the night sky, while others were busy playing cards or engrossed in conversation. Could there ever be a better night than this, he wondered. Rigel drifted off into a deep peaceful sleep filled with happiness.

3.   THE JINX RETURNS

On the third day at sea there was an incident that would give all involved a feeling of impending doom. Rigel heard his master and another crewman talking in hushed tones and he could tell by the way they were talking that something was terribly wrong. "There's a fire in the coal bunker that we can't put out. Do not breathe a word of this to anyone as there would be panic!" We'll call for the fireboats as soon as we reach New York". Rigel didn't understand what his master said to the crewman, but he didn't like seeing him upset and he tried to console him as best he could.

Rigel is given a big hug and is comforted by his master's confident voice, "there, there, nothing to worry about, just a minor problem, nothing we can't handle." He sounded more like he was trying to convince himself rather than his faithful dog.

The morning of April 14th was uneventful which after the previous day was a welcome change. Rigel stayed on deck for most of the day looking over the side railing and wishing he would be allowed to swim.

That would be the one factor that would make this the most perfect assignment. Little did he know that later that night on one of the worst nights in history he would get his wish!

There were more children on deck that day and Rigel found himself entertaining a large group of them. They made him perform a whole repertoire of tricks like sit-up, play dead, roll over, then they had him fetching their toys. But Rigel didn't mind, he loved children and had as much fun as they did. The children were called to dinner but not before promising him table scraps. Later that night they kept their promise and Rigel was rewarded with a leftover steak dinner. This had been a relaxing day for him filled with playing, eating and sleeping, which was good because that evening he would have to summon all the strength he could muster!

4. NIGHT OF TERROR

Nighttime came swiftly and it was time for his work shift. Rigel noticed some strange looking shapes in the water. He had never seen the likes of them before, they looked like mountains made of snow. The men in the crow's nest noticed them also, unfortunately, it was too late. "Iceberg, iceberg dead ahead!" they shouted. The first officer reacted as fast as he could but the huge liner couldn't, and they collided. There was a bang then a long scraping noise. Large chunks of ice fell on the top deck. The event went mostly unnoticed by the passengers. The few that were on deck when it happened didn't seem concerned at all. After all, it was the unsinkable Titanic, what could possibly happen?

A few started to have snowball fights with the snow. This looked like great fun to Rigel and he ran to join in the action. At first, they only threw the snowballs over his head. But then they started to throw to him and he amazed everyone by catching each one in his mouth.

At about the same time, Captain Smith is notified about the accident.

He consults with the ships' designer and learns the sad truth that his ship is doomed and will sink in less than two hours. With no time to spare, he calls passengers to the few lifeboats with women and children boarding first. Some lifeboats leave dangerously overcrowded, some are half-empty. Yet, most still aren't taking the accident seriously.

By 1:20, the great ship is listing badly and passengers are beginning to panic. Suddenly, a foreign speaking man forces his way through the crowd carrying two small boys. As he approaches the rail, one by one, he throws the children over the side! Rigel is horrified and runs to the railing to see where they landed and is relieved to see that they safely reached the open arms of a lifeboat crewman.

There is much confusion, people are running back and forth, there is crying and yelling, gun shots and rockets are being fired into the air. It is a night of terror unlike most of us will ever know!

Rigel finds his beloved master in a state of shock. "Oh, Rigel, what have we done, what have we done?" he whispers over and over. Rigel tries to console him but it's no use. Slowly his master walks away to assist with the lifeboats and that's the last Rigel sees of him.

Off in the distance, he hears his friends, the musicians playing and he runs

off to warn them. He barks a warning and tries to get the band to follow him.

They call to him, "Rigel come here boy, hey I know we're in trouble but we

have a job to do and you have a job to do too. You have to try to help as many

people as you can, go on now, go help those people."

Rigel seemed to understand and as he runs off, the band breaks into a

comforting hymn.

It's very late, around 2:00 am, the Titanic is in it's death throes. The ship starts tilting upward and Rigel finds himself sliding down the deck!

People around him are screaming and holding onto the railing for dear life!

Scared and confused he jumps into what has always been a safe haven for him, the water.

It's colder than he imagined but not unbearable. Just then the ship points upward like a giant black finger reaching for the sky. Within minutes the unsinkable liner slipped gracefully beneath the waves.

5.   THE RESCUE

The lifeboats had all rowed a safe distance and all that was left in the water where the Titanic once rested was a large debris field and many people. At first, Rigel searches for his master but his search is in vain. He had no way of knowing that he went down with the ship. He couldn't bear the sound of anyone hurt or in agony and on this fateful night, he was surrounded by hundreds all crying and begging for help. He looked around, where could he take them where there was no land, no ship and the lifeboats were getting further and further away! He tried to help as many as he could by pulling them onto floating debris but soon the chorus of crying is joined by the wailing of a very sad dog.

"Rigel, Rigel, come here," it was a familiar voice of one of the young crewman

who is trying to swim. He grabs onto Rigel's back and is brought to a collapsible

lifeboat that was left behind. There are quite a few men on this boat and they

pull the young man onboard. Soon the water is silent and Rigel decides to

follow the lifeboats thinking he would find his master on one of them.

The survivors in the lifeboats look back occasionally and try to make out the figure that is swimming behind them. "It's not a person, I think it's a dog. Maybe it's that big black one that was always hanging around the bridge", one of them thinks out loud. At any rate, they had more important tasks to worry about namely rowing to the rescue ship the "Carpathia" that was steaming full speed into the same icefield that sank their ship! There is a light in the distance and all head towards it.

The survivors were all exhausted, half frozen from exposure, distraught and still in shock. It had been three long hours, which to the people in the boats seemed like an eternity. The Carpathia comes into view, it is moving slowly looking for survivors. The first three lifeboats are brought alongside and rescued.

The Carpathia moves along to find other lifeboats, but unfortunately they don't realize that a lifeboat has drifted dangerously close to the bow. This goes unnoticed by everyone except Rigel! The boat members are exhausted and too weak to shout out any warnings. Rigel bravely swims between the Carpathia and the hapless lifeboat and commandingly announces his position! The officers are alerted by the sound of a bass bark coming from the water. They look over the bow to see an accident about to happen and the captain orders, "engines stopped"!

Everyone is saved and after the lifeboat is emptied, great care is taken to bring the hero dog onboard. He seemed no worse for wear and with a mighty shake succeeds in showering everyone close with salt water. What proved to be fatal for so many was nothing more than a midnight swim to him!

6. A NEW BEGINNING

More lifeboats come within view and Rigel can hardly contain his enthusiasm as he runs back and forth barking orders. A young seaman named John is instantly attached to him, "Oh what a beautiful dog, where on earth did you come from?" A Titanic crewman answered, "That's Rigel, he was our mascot. His master went down with the ship." Captain Rostron is beginning to lose his patience with the eager to help mascot and tells the young seaman, since you like the dog so much take him below, he's yours!"

50

"Did you hear that, your mine," and he gives the dog a big hug.

Happily, the two go below to his quarters. "Well you had quite an adventure, didn't you? Wait here, I'll be right back." He returns shortly with food and water and begins to towel dry his new companion.

The nightmare was over and now it was time for a good night's sleep. It wasn't a restful sleep though, as images of the sinking ship kept coming back to haunt him. John felt bad for his new friend and invited Rigel to sleep on the end of the bed. There with his new master comforting him he finally drifted off into sleep.

The rescue ship was filled with sadness the morning after. Many of the Carpathia's passengers tried to make the new guests feel at home. Some made clothing out of extra blankets, others offered hot drinks or a shoulder to cry on. Though most were still in shock and bitter, many welcomed the friendliness and kind words.

Rigel made his way around the deck and scanned the crowd for any familiar

faces. His band friends weren't on board and neither was his original master,

but there were the children who loved him. He ran to greet them and they

showered him with affection.

Just then a tall, elegantly dressed woman walks up to him. She leans down

to pet him and exclaims, " You made it, didn't you?" "Well good for you fella,

good for you! Rigel happily wags his tail in appreciation.

Thousands were in New York awaiting the little rescue ship including the many reporters eager for the shocking and tearful stories each survivor could surely tell. The Titanic survivors slowly walked down the gangplank including the three surviving dogs. Rigel wasn't the only dog to survive the sinking, a Pekinese and a Pomeranian were smuggled on board lifeboats hidden in their owner's coats. This shocked and horrified the reporters. "Do you mean to say that dogs lived when so many people died" a reporter asked angrily.

Rigel's new owner stepped forward, "I can't speak for the lives of those little dogs, but I can speak for this one. This dog wasn't on a lifeboat, he swam in that freezing water for over three hours saving people all the way" He deserves to live!" The reporter is amazed and calls John over for the full details.

Their stay in New York was a fairly short one. Carpathia had to finish the voyage, which was interrupted, to do their rescue mission. Thousands returned to see the little steamer off. There were throngs of cheering people, banners of congratulations and many dozens of small escort boats.

This was a bigger display of affection than what the Titanic had received!

They had all come to pay homage in grand style and Rigel was right there where he belonged, on a ship full of heroes"

About the Author

Christine Jamesson had been reading and researching the Titanic tragedy for many years when she found a fascinating but little known article about Rigel. In 1990 she sent a movie script about the Titanic to a producer and although he wasn't interested in the script, he was very interested in Rigel and suggested she write a story about him. First published as an electronic book it has now been revised and updated with 35 full color drawings.

Ms. Jamesson has a paralegal degree and enjoys research projects, gardening and collecting antiquities. This is her third published book in addition to several articles and poems.

LaVergne, TN USA
22 February 2010
173888LV00002B